Moribund Tales

Moribund Tales

Erik Hofstatter

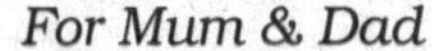

For Mum & Dad

Contents

Internal Abduction

HE night was filled with noise, an equal concoction of rapid sounds and vibrations described as music. It stirred the pain in my brain from the previous night of excessive indulgence. The foundations of every home and office building for miles around were shaking from the thunderous bass emanating from the local nightclub. Two women, in their early twenties, emerged from inside this modern temple of Dionysus. I made a point of brushing against the pretty brunette who was engaged in hysterical conversation.

The medieval city of Rochester that had once been a prestigious and historically significant location was now reduced to nothing more than a vulture's hunting ground. The streets were tyrannized by lowlifes and hooligans. No one was safe anymore. The local citizens barricaded themselves inside their homes, not venturing out once the darkness swooped over the city and the night time mob arrived to indulge in all kinds of perverse activities. Times were spiralling out of control. The inhabitants, initiated to more desperate measures, were willing to sell their own souls for profit.

My eccentric roommate, Sean, told me about a local medical lab where he submitted himself for prescription drug experimentation. The number of students choosing to follow that path was increasing daily. Of course, it was a risk to your health, but it paid well. We live in challenging times.

I turned right into a shady road, towards the location of my experimental trial. The late night appointment had already made me a little suspicious. According to Sean's instructions, the medical lab was situated behind an industrial park in a deserted alley. In this deranged city, stricken with poverty and fear, most folk were willing to commit murder for a handful of change. I hastened my step as the smell of paranoia invaded the atmosphere. Someone was watching me.

At my feet, I observed an undisturbed puddle reflecting the full moon that was decorating the heavens. Before me, an abandoned wasteland stretched out into the distance. I felt invisible knots gripping my insides, pulling them tight. A sudden tremor resurrected the still water from its contented slumber, making it evident that something was on my trail.

The area was populated with twisted vagabonds. I hesitated and extracted my mobile, dialling imaginary digits. "Sean!" I said flamboyantly. "Wait for me outside the building. I'm almost there." I said these words as confidently as I could in order to warn any potential assailants that there was someone expecting me. The fact I was out of credit meant the conversation was rather one sided.

The desire to turn my head suddenly became irresistible. Scaling the scenery behind me, I listened ardently for any suspicious activity. Saliva was absent from my dry mouth. I felt my heartbeat quicken as my eyes searched for something dangerously close. My instinct was warning me that something meant me harm.

I suddenly collided with something massive. A cloth that was soaked with some kind of narcotic was pushed into my face. The desired effect was immediate. The fumes paralyzed my brain, and my knees crumbled as I floated into unconsciousness.

The water from a broken pipe above my head gradually revived me. I was on the ground. The earth was damp and arctic. Pain played with my mind in a staccato rhythm. Crawling on debilitated knees, I tried to find something to help me to my feet. Although my view was still obscured by the effects of the drugs, I came to realise that I was in the curve of a murky, unlit road.

Whoever inflicted this upon me must have dragged me into the darkness. Why? For what purpose?

My black winter coat and denim jeans were drenched while my frame shivered beyond control. If only the raging agony in my temples would cease! What the hell has happened to me?!

Visions of the assault gradually began skulking back. Yes, I was attacked... but not in a traditional manner. The assailants didn't demand my valuables at gun-or knife-point. I was shocked to discover that none of my possessions had been stolen. My mobile and wallet were still in my pocket. What was the point? What were they after?

Terror seized my limbs. The trauma of the ordeal clawed at my senses. Going to the lab in this condition was inadvisable. The logical destination was the police station, but what viable fruit would my revelation bear? I was attacked, but there were no signs of physical damage.

I felt an unfamiliar sensation deep within. Something *was* missing. Something *did* assault me. The motive remained a puzzle. Who were these fiends?

The city's mechanical fumes contaminated the atmosphere while I limped along the foul sidewalk. The night chilled me to the core as a gang of dubious adolescents conspired on the corner. The nausea increased as a metallic flavour invaded my mouth. Was this the aftermath of the toxic chemical I was compelled to inhale?

Perspiration rose to the surface of my features as I vomited over the side of a bridge into the river below. The drivers that passed me made rude gestures or honked in amusement, miscalculating my mysterious symptoms for those of an ordinary drunkard. My determination faded, and oblivion snatched me as I collapsed to the ground.

I was woken by an intense light being shined in my eyes, forcing me to open them. And there was an overwhelming scent of bleach. Had the monsters returned to dispose of me?

A man in a white coat positioned himself on the edge of the bed. The protruding bags under his eyes betrayed his antiqued age.

"I'm Dr. Mahapatra. How are you feeling?"

"Where am I?"

"St. Margaret's hospital," he replied. "You were found on Rochester Bridge."

The memory of my unexpected collapse gradually resurfaced. I wondered if these thoughts would help me recall further details about the attack. This might be a blessing in disguise, considering whoever assaulted me still lurked within the city. What if they ambushed someone else?

"You know," the doctor began, in a concerned tone, "a man in your condition should really take better care of himself."

This declaration puzzled me. What did he mean? I was in sensational shape. I'm in the peak of health. Illness never plagues me for any length of time.

"What exactly are you referring to, doctor?"

He levelled his eyes to mine and countered with a question. "You mean you're unaware of your condition?"

This doctor was absurd. "Yes, I'm completely oblivious to my condition!"

"Well, according to our medical report, it seems your sudden collapse was caused by exhaustion and a lack of rest. The procedure you underwent is serious. It takes time before your body can heal and adjust."

I observed the pale ceiling above me and shook my head in disbelief. What on earth was he talking about?

"I don't understand," I said. "I haven't had any surgery!"

The doctor appeared equally mystified. "You do realize that one of your kidneys has been removed? And judging by the softness of the scar it happened very recently, perhaps only hours ago. You should have been in hospital for at least a week."

I felt the blood drain from my face.

"What's the name of the hospital that performed the operation?" the Doctor asked. "I'm rather concerned about your situation. How did you end up on that bridge?"

My overloaded brain was striving to process all the information that it had just obtained. The doctor's features turned from concern to horror as he noticed the shock on my face.

Instinctively, I lifted my hospital gown and beheld an elongated scar spreading from my right to my dorsum. It looked raw and sloppy. An operation performed impetuously. At last, I was able to comprehend the full purpose of the assault. They were not hunting for money. They were searching for internal organs. My god! What have they done to me?

Last Straw of Humanity

THE cries always increased at night. Always. I knew what lay beyond the door. What I didn't understand was... why? Father never explained his reasons. One thing I did know for sure was that if he ever caught me anywhere near the cellar... he would kill me.

I've ignored his cruelty for the past fourteen years, but no more. I can no longer, with good conscience, ignore what is under the floorboards.

As usual, I was sick with fear as compassion invaded my mind. Nevertheless, I must obey what my heart asks of me.

My hands began to tremble as I descended the uneven stairs. The only source of light available to me was the tiny candle in my hand. Darkness devoured everything around me as I heard the unmistakeable sound of nails scratching at the walls.

There was a door in front of me. I pressed my ear against it and listened intently. Strange wailing came from within. My father's callousness was beyond belief. No human could ignore such pleading, but my Father's heart was immune to empathy.

Out of the darkness, a powerful hand emerged and grabbed me by the collar. I was thrown backwards. Everything blurred. When my sight returned, I could see the savage face of my father looking down at me. I was petrified.

He took a handful of hair and began to drag me towards the stairs. I tried to resist, but my Father's hands were like iron clamps. I couldn't break his hold.

"What did I tell you, boy?" I held my breath.

"This is for your own good!" he said as he removed his belt. "I told you to stay outta there!"

I sobbed. My tears only served to fuel Father's anger.

He was a massive man. All the endless hours spent slaving in the mines had given him a robust and frightening physique. I wept with every blow as rage and disappointment burned in his merciless eyes. Then he stopped.

That night, pain kept me awake. As much as I wanted to help, my own safety came first. My death would be of no use to anyone.

The following night, after supper, I made Father some coffee. He stood in front of the blazing fireplace, lighting his pipe. The smoke created a bitter taste in my mouth. He took the cup gratefully and offered me a chair.

"Father," I began, tentatively. "You know you can't leave him down there in the cellar forever."

"He is an abomination, son. Work of the devil. God would never create such a monster. You know I only keep him alive out of pity."

"Why don't you kill him if you hate him so much?"

Father shifted in his chair and took a sip of his drink. After wiping his mouth on his sleeve, he replied, "I thought about it, but I couldn't bring myself to do it."

"He is a human being!" I protested. "You can't keep him imprisoned forever!"

He gave me a sharp glance. "You'd better watch that tone, boy. He's against nature! He's against the bible! I'm telling you he is the devil's minion. If I ever catch you near the door again, it will be an axe in my hand, not a belt. End of discussion."

My mind was made up. I would do it that night, and he wouldn't stop me.

While Father slept, I took hold of my grey rucksack and packed as many rations as I could find. Then I saw the shotgun resting above the fireplace. I took it down and laid it beside my bag.

Creeping upstairs, taking caution with every step, I tried not to let them reveal my presence. Peeking through a crack in the doorway, I saw my father. His face was calm and peaceful. He was snoring obliviously.

I licked my lower lip and reached for his keys. My heart plunged into my stomach as he suddenly shifted. For a moment, I thought he would grab my hand and chop it off, but he remained immobile. After liberating them, I hurried away. The cellar was my next destination.

I descended the stairs. If Father was incapable of mercy, it was my duty to find it for him. A sudden sense of shame penetrated my mind. If only I'd found my courage earlier.

As I took the rusty keys out of my pocket, a sudden wave of anticipation hit me. I unlocked the door and removed the heavy chains. I could hear the same distant wails.

Once inside, I saw nothing but darkness. Cautiously, I ventured forwards. There was a disfigured shape cowering in the corner.

"It's okay, George, I'm your brother." I whispered softly.

As I got closer, I observed that something was terribly wrong. His face remained hidden, but the structure of his body alarmed me. It appeared that his right arm was mutated into some kind of pendulous stub, while his legs were horrendously misshapen.

I put the candle down in front me and took a step towards him. He sprang up violently and knocked it over. He'd been kept in the dark for so many years that his eyes were sensitive to direct light.

Luckily, the candle didn't go out. I picked it up and placed it as far away from him as I could. I turned and sensed him crawling towards me. His movement seemed primitive and beastly.

"Are your legs broken?" I asked. "Can you walk?"

I repressed a scream as his face was illuminated by the flame. My brother was deformed, mutilated beyond human recognition.

His left eye hung significantly lower than the other, and as he turned his head, I could see that his skull was twice the size of a regular human being. His mouth was at an angle, with the upper lip missing. The teeth he had left were all rotten.

Now I understood why my father kept him in the cellar all these years. He was unwilling to kill his son, but he also knew that society would never accept him.

I realized it was my duty to save him. If Father had his wicked way, George was destined to rot in this filth until the end of his days.

Walking over to him, I grabbed his arm and helped him up. George staggered, but willingly limped forward towards the door.

"You have to be quiet," I whispered. "If father catches us, I'll probably end up in here with you."

We climbed the stairs but were far from subtle. I was convinced that, with all the commotion, Father was going to discover us.

I retrieved my rucksack and made for the door. Turning towards my brother, in triumph, I expected to see the joyous face of a man granted his freedom. All I saw was pain and suffering.

The truth hit me like a thousand knives piercing me all at once. I swallowed hard because I knew what I had to do.

I pointed my finger at the night sky and said, "Look at that beautiful moon."

As George stood, captivated by the illuminating satellite, I slowly pulled out my

father's shotgun and aimed it at his head.
"I'm sorry, Brother."

Chaperone

WAS blind when I woke. The tips of my fingers explored the surrounding ground. It was humid. The smooth grass tickled my palms. There was a peculiar aroma in the air; a fusion of composting leaves and fresh rain. The moist earth beneath my bones indicated that I was in a garden, park or a forest, although I heard no other voices.

I tried to stand, but my head collided with a solid surface. Cursing, I raised my sightless eyes towards the heavens and touched the protruding obstacle. It was a tree.

My mind possessed no recollection of how I had arrived here. Crawling on my hands and knees, I examined the nearby area, searching vigorously for possible clues. Perhaps there was an empty whiskey bottle which would explain my amnesia. Perhaps I got drunk and passed out?

I stood up from the terra firma and massaged my aching scalp. I inhaled deeply, the jagged oxygen slicing through my lungs like a knife through butter.

My surroundings were deprived of life, except for me and the tree. Perhaps even the tree was dead? My eyes could not tell. There was no other sound. No birds, traffic or rustling leaves. I was alone, it seemed.

My heart sank when I became aware of my vulnerable state. What was I going to do? How would I get home? How did I end up here in the first place? All these questions swam through my mind like shoaling fishes.

I stumbled upon a broken branch. Lifting it up, I tested its durability and length against the tree. This would serve as my cane. Armed with my new discovery, I started walking. I did not know where, as my current position was still a mystery to me, but I was bound to encounter a helpful soul somewhere along the way.

I walked briskly, feeling my way with the stick along the slippery grass, unsure of the course of my unplanned journey. It was then, from out of the darkness, I heard an inaudible whisper.

"Who are you?" I called out. "Please! I am lost! I need help!"

"You do not have to travel far, my friend," a soothing voice replied.

"Follow the hill for half a mile. When you reach the summit, I will guide you the rest of the way."

There was a trace of melancholy in the voice that I knew I had to obey. I was lost in the wilderness of God knows where; perhaps *he* held some knowledge of my whereabouts?

I heeded his advice and continued my journey towards the hilltop. I hoped my mysterious benefactor would be true to his word and help me. As I strolled, I desperately tried to recall what had happened to me. My last memory was of a violent argument with my wife, Esther.

She has a lover. I even know his name.

Esther refers to him as her "silver wolf". He would have been a silver corpse if I wasn't restricted by our modern laws and mechanized society. Alas, I was born in the wrong century.

The passion between us perished long ago, but for the sake of our marriage, I chose to ignore her infidelity.

That proved to be a difficult task as the desire to butcher her grew daily. I convinced myself she seduced him because for the daughters of Eve. . . seduction and betrayal are in their blood.

* * *

The bottle of whiskey had hissed in my ear, urging me to confront her about the affair and be done with it, once and for all. No more humiliation.

She barged in through the door, her cheeks flushed from sex that should have been with me, her husband.

My senses were dulled by the liquor, as she brushed past and greeted me with blissful ignorance. She felt superior, I'm sure.

Following her into the kitchen, armed with the bottle in one hand and a clenched fist in the other, I halted in the doorframe. I licked my blistered lips and felt the absence of saliva in my dry mouth.

"You look a bit sweaty, darling. Had a rigorous workout?"

Esther flung the fridge door shut and gave me a crawl-back-into-your-bottle kind of look. She proceeded to ignore my intoxicated self and carried on with her endeavours in silence. That pissed me off.

It's bad enough when someone argues back, and you want to silence them by ripping out their tongue, but when you're met with silence like you don't exist... that is an entirely different kind of insult.

"Did you hear me, you fucking harlot?"

Esther faced me at last, a furious fire burning in her ocean-blue eyes.

"Why are you still here? I told you last week to grab your shit and get the fuck out of my flat!"

I staggered away from the door and placed the bottle on our marble credence.

"Because I'm still in love with you," I pleaded, even though my fingers itched for her throat.

Esther flicked her curly hair in annoyance.

"In case it has escaped your notice, I'm not in love with *you*. In fact, I never loved you," she said, draining my rapidly depleting ego. "I need a real man, see?

Her laughter echoed through our spacious kitchen. That was the final straw. I couldn't restrain the titan that was my temper any longer.

"You little whore!" I said through gritted teeth, as my backhand connected with her foul mouth.

My sense of pride returned as I watched her trembling in the corner.

"That's right, slut, you will learn your place."

I turned around and took a swig from the bottle. While I was quenching my thirst, Esther reached for a huge kitchen knife and defiantly pointed it in my face.

"The kitten's got claws, eh?"

Esther kept waving the knife at me as she backed away like a cornered beast.

"Get away from me... you lowlife!"

I stopped and tilted my head to the side.

"Let's find out how sharp your claws really are, little kitty."

* * *

The grass felt cold under my feet as I continued ascending the monstrous hill. My nostrils detected a swift change in atmosphere, as drops of rain started falling like thousands of sharpened arrows.

The penetrating rain drenched my clothes to the last thread. I shivered, but pressed on. I was determined to reach the summit and hear the voice of my mysterious guide once more. But would he truly lead me home?

* * *

There was fear in her eyes. This gave me an enormous sense of victory. I took a run-up and managed to land a kick in her ribs as she made a feeble slash at my foot but missed.

I needed to refuel, so I left her there, sobbing.

As I took another greedy gulp of whiskey, I heard movement behind me. I whipped around. It was then that I felt the knife being driven deep into my flesh.

Esther's eyes bore into mine. "Take that, you bullying fuck."

Blood dripped down from my abdomen, decorating the kitchen linoleum. I tried to fight back, but my knees crumbled and I collapsed.

* * *

I reached the top of the treacherous mound and wiped the rain out of my wind-beaten face. It was then that I felt the warm breath in my right ear. It was shallow and hard to hear, but undeniably... someone stood beside me.

"Who's there?"

"I am your Chaperone," a voice replied, with perfect equilibrium. "I'm here to escort you to your new home."

"New home?" I asked. "What are you talking about?"

"I am here to take you to a place where those who enter have abandoned all hope."

This was when the truth finally dawned on me... I was dead.

Gears of Repentance

 SHUDDERED as a sense of dread washed over me. There was a darkness that was intent on invading my consciousness. I tried to shove the sentiment aside, but I was unable to shake the fear that haunted me whenever the moon was high.

I lived in a small village whose population has been halved by the Black Death. For some reason, it took my parents, but I was spared. Most of my teens were dominated by hard labour and the consumption of vast quantities of mead. I lived a shallow existence until she entered my life and changed everything.

God had blessed me with an angel.

I met her on Execution Rock in Bulgaria. The Tsar had sentenced a vagrant to death, and we were required to witness the event. The condemned vagabond was on his knees in front of him, soiling himself as he begged for his life. I watched with the rest of the crowd as a hand was waved and the man was pushed into the Yantra.

The black river had another victim to devour.

I held my breath and turned away. It was then that her ocean-blue eyes met with mine. For a moment, she distracted me from the screams that would haunt my dreams for weeks to come.

The following evening, I tried to drown my melancholy in the nearest public house. The establishment was crowded, but I still managed to find my one and only. She had a voice that was soft and sweeter than the mead that no longer interested me. Her name was Ingra, and she was beautiful. From the moment she sat down beside me, the two of us were in love.

This was seven years ago.

I strolled through the shadows to my humble dwelling. Part of me hoped she wouldn't come tonight, but I knew that was wishful thinking. My intuition was confirmed when I saw a candle burning on my windowsill.

I unlocked the door and stepped inside, not daring to breathe. The flame was the only source of light available to me. As my pupils adjusted to the murkiness, I spotted a shadow crouching in the corner. It was her.

She was wearing the same blood-stained rag that she had worn on that fateful day.

Her face was buried in hands that were forever coloured red. It was my fault. I had led her to this fate.

Ingra raised her shaved head and stared at me with those forget-me-not eyes.

"Take a good look at me!" she said, bitterly. "My blood is on you."

I lowered my gaze in shame, searching for words that would never be enough.

"I know I failed you," I said, my voice heavy with guilt, "but you betrayed me first."

Ingra remained silent.

"How could you give up on us?"

"I waited for you to change," she replied. "You never did. I loved you more than life itself, but your flaws became too hard to bear. You might think that my decision to abandon you was an act of betrayal, but it was you who pushed me towards such an action."

"I cried for you every night for a year."

"I don't want to hear any of your excuses. You are responsible for my death. For that, I will make you pay."

The flame blew out, and she was gone.

Ingra was right, what happened was my fault, but as far as I was concerned, she died the day she walked out on me.

I knew she was planning to leave the moment our eyes met. They were empty, cold and distant. I sat down and drank some mead, faking my ignorance.

"I feel as if we've grown apart," she said as she sat in the chair beside me. "When we kiss, I no longer have butterflies in my belly."

"We've been together for five years," I replied. "The thrill was bound to diminish."

This was it, the beginning of the end. I had to ask the question.

"Are you thinking of leaving me?"

"No, Grigor, I'd never do that. You're my soul mate." She looked away. I could see a conflicted look on her face. "I just... need your permission for something."

I raised my eyebrows. "Permission?"

"I've started to develop feelings for another man. There is this attraction between us that I can no longer fight. I'm asking you to let us lay together for one night."

I should have killed her there and then. How could she advocate such madness?

"What do you take me for?!" I raged, slamming my fist on the table. "How could you even approach me with this atrocity? Did you honestly think I would support your desire to copulate with another man?"

Ingra's face was solemn. She remained silent while I gave in to my temper.

"Why did you even seek my permission? Why not just go ahead and do it?"

"Calm down, Grigor, please! I asked because I don't want to lose you! I thought you would understand and see how it would benefit our relationship."

Ingra reached for my hand, but I moved it away.

"Please, Grigor, look at me."

"I'm only going to say this once," I declared. "If you're prepared to sacrifice our many years together for the sake of one meaningless night with some peasant, then you have my permission to fulfil your selfish desire. Just remember that should you give in to this temptation, it will be the end for us."

"But—"

I gently pressed my finger to her lips. "The choice is yours."

The harlot left me that night. I was devastated. Deep down, I was convinced that her love wouldn't allow her to leave. How wrong could I be? Her departure took a week to sink in. I kept asking myself... why?

How could I not be enough? She was my second self; my immortal beloved. I tried not to think of her, but there was so much to miss. I found it hard to live without the sound of her voice and the way her eyes lit up as she laughed over the silliest of things.

I collapsed to my knees as an army of tears assaulted my cheeks. I begged God for his guidance and a sign of what I should do next. Loneliness had a hold of me. All I wanted was the comfort of her touch. Every night, I would drink until I passed out. This was the only way I could numb the pain of my broken heart.

After eight months of silence, my prayers were answered. I received a note. I immediately recognized the child-like handwriting as Ingra's. I was suspicious at first, having received no prior correspondence. My pride almost made me throw it into the hearth, but curiosity prevailed.

I sat down and searched my feelings. Yes, my heart still yearned for her company, but I would not seek it out. If I'm to be denied her love, then I should at least keep my dignity.

The note was short, yet direct. "I miss you. Can we meet? My father will tell you where to find me."

A range of emotions surged through my mind. I had feelings of pain, hate, love and revenge. I ripped the note, twice, before tossing it into the fire. Why did she want to see me now? Did she honestly think I would take her back after another man had been inside her?

I wanted to tell her that I had never stopped loving her, not for a second. Those words were meant to be whispered in her ear as I held her close to me. I had waited so long for this very moment, yet no matter how much I wanted to turn this fantasy into reality, the bitterness in my heart forbade it.

She wasn't worthy of mine or anyone else's love. Ingra had betrayed me and had to be stopped before she could inflict this kind of pain on someone else. I'd walked through hell and back because of her. I deserved some justice.

I decided to go to church and seek the advice of Father Todor. I was going to lie to a man of the cloth in order to get my revenge on a former lover.

"Ah, Grigor, my son, what brings you here?"

"I've come to see you because I am troubled. I witnessed something terrible last night, and I need to tell someone."

"What is it?"

"It's about Ingra, Father. I've discovered her secret. She hid it well, but last night I uncovered the truth!"

"What have you found out?"

"I was plagued with insomnia, so I went for a walk in the woods. I heard voices and decided to investigate. It was then that I recognized her naked figure. She was dancing with some other wenches; they were all nude and chanting words in a language I'd never heard before. That was when it occurred to me that she must be a witch!"

"This is grave news indeed, my son. I know her father. He is an honest, god-fearing man. Are you absolutely sure of this?"

"Yes, Father. When we lived together, she used to go out at night. I never knew where, but now I know!"

Father Todor was a superstitious man who despised witches. That was why I went to him. His prejudice would ensure that my story would be taken seriously.

"The Devil placed his mark upon her inner thigh. You have to believe me, Father. She is the devil's whore. I'm scared she will come after me!"

"Yes, yes of course," mumbled the priest, "I will inform the Tsar at once."

Ingra was seized that very evening on suspicion of witchcraft. She was tortured until she confessed. The Tsar sentenced her to death without a trial.

Next morning, the villagers gathered on Execution Rock. As with every woman accused of such a crime, she would burn on the pyre.

"HERE COMES THE WITCH! BURN HER! BURN HER! BURN THE WITCH!"

Two of the Tsar's guards dragged Ingra towards the fire and tied her to the stake. She was a frightening sight to behold. Her golden hair had been shaved off while all her teeth had been pulled out. They were the souvenirs of the torture she had endured.

As Father Todor prayed for her damned soul, the villagers bayed for blood. I threw the first torch, and many more followed. "I'm pregnant," she screamed, but her words were lost beneath the hate of the angry mob. Her eyes that were once ocean-blue turned into an ocean of sorrow.

I wept as I'm weeping now. She didn't deserve to die. I had no right to seal her fate in the way I did. I knew in my heart, why her ghost kept visiting. It was her turn to be thirsty for vengeance.

The night after she'd threatened me, her ghost returned. I thought she was only allowed to visit me once a month. Why was she back so soon? Was she here to take my soul to the underworld?

"Are you here to kill me, Ingra?"

"Why would I want that?"

"Then what do you want? Why are you here? What is the purpose of your visits?"

"I know what I asked of you was irrational and unfair, but was it worth condemning me to death?"

I shook my head in frustration. "It was the Tsar, not me! I tried, Ingra! The longer I waited, the more I missed you. But you never came back! You wrote a note, but you never knocked on my door! I thought you loved me, but you left me for another man! I couldn't live with that. You were mine and mine alone, so I made sure that if I couldn't have you, no one else could."

She fell silent for a moment. "There was never anyone else."

"I'm supposed to believe that?"

"Yes. I was faithful until the end. It was your child that was growing in my womb as I burned to death."

Ingra's tears flowed down her cheeks as she continued with her confession.

"You see, the day I left you, I went for a walk in the forest and thought about the last few years. I'd rushed into our relationship, and even though I loved you, I was confused about what I wanted. I started suffocating through the intensity of our union! I was confused. I thought that if I slept with another man the feeling might depart. I saw the pain in your eyes the day I asked for your permission, so I left and secretly moved back in with my father. I started the rumours that I had moved into the next village. I needed time to figure out what I really wanted from you... and from myself. Then, I finally realized how rare and wonderful our relationship truly was. I made the decision to come back to you, only to discover that you had made a decision of your own... to have me killed."

"I didn't want that! I just didn't know what else to do!"

Having made her confession, Ingra had gone. She had passed over into the next realm. I bowed my head. At last, I knew what I had to do.

I ran out into the cold night, through the village with its dogs that barked at the moon. I raced as fast as I could up the hill until I finally reached Execution Rock. I crept to the edge and stared into the black abyss. This was what Ingra's ghost desired. Of course, in my heart, I knew it was my conscience that had haunted me each and every night.

My reckoning had come. I closed my eyes and prayed.

If faith divides us, death will unite us.

Soul Reflection

HE ground floor of an old apartment block had been baptised by fire. A senile occupant had drifted unwittingly into slumber and thus, a solitary flame from a single candle had turned into an angry inferno. The scent of charred flesh was soaked into the foundations of the building, ensuring its vacancy for years to come.

On the top floor, inside a modest room, a frightened youth begged not to be involved in his uncle's villainous scheme.

"Please!" Peter pleaded, his eyes slowly filling up with tears. "Don't make me!"

"Stop being such a sissy!" Frank hissed as he shot his twelve year old nephew a malefic glance.

"I'm scared!" Peter said, bowing his head like a condemned prisoner.

Frank Payne's heart was heavy with guilt. *Maybe I should reconsider, he thought. The boy is innocent.* His dark desires prevailed in the end.

"It won't hurt," he said, reassuringly. "You have my word."

"What do I have to do?" Peter asked, his voice trembling.

"All I need is a witness," Frank answered. "You won't have to do anything at all."

Peter remained silent for a moment. "And what will you do, Uncle?" he asked, voicing the question that his troubled mind wanted answered.

"Wait and see. Tonight. . . you will understand everything."

Peter turned his head and looked out the window. The night had devoured everything in its path. He shivered. His thoughts were in turmoil.

The child's oblivious dreams were disrupted by the icy hand that shook him awake.

"Get up, Pete!" Frank's voice was full of excitement. "I need you now."

"What time is it?"

"Time to get up. Now get dressed and hurry up about it!"

The boy staggered into the living room and gave a tiny gasp. The walls were decorated with unknown encryptions. A skilfully carved table lay in the middle of the room with an antique mirror dominating its centre. A single candle shone in front of it.

Frank kneeled and put down a sacrificial dagger. "Tonight, my boy. . . we shall attempt to get a glimpse of my soul through the mirror."

Peter was transfixed, his mind chaotic.

"Come closer," Frank whispered. His nephew took several unsteady steps towards him. "From now on, be quiet and obey my every command. Stand behind me and don't speak. You hear me, boy?"

He nodded, signalling his understanding.

The temperature of the room dropped, creating a chilly atmosphere. The flat was already cold from the damp that was hiding in the walls. To Peter, it almost appeared as if time stood still. The only person that existed was his uncle kneeling in front of the peculiar mirror, gazing upon his reflection with murderous intensity.

Suddenly, without a word, Frank picked up the ceremonial dagger and slashed himself across his palm.

Peter twitched and almost let out a scream of protest as he saw how heavily the open wound was bleeding. Frank calmly smeared his bloody hand across the eyes of his own reflection.

"Uncle, please stop this madness!" Peter whined. "You're scaring me!"

And then... he saw it.

The youth trembled and fell back against the wall. "Look!" he exclaimed. "Your reflection..."

The candle had illuminated the other Frank's determined grimace.

Peter mustered the sum of his courage and leapt over his uncle. He knew he had to break the spell and knock the mirror over.

A hand reached up and grabbed his wrist, holding it in an iron clamp. "No! Don't touch it!" Frank snapped. "I won't let you interfere!"

The boy looked at his enchanted uncle and then back to the mirror. He weighed his options and decided to knock over the candle instead.

"I can't watch any longer!" Peter screamed as he dived for the light and extinguished the flame between his petite fingers.

"You imbecile!" Frank seized his nephew by the collar and shook him frantically. "Do you even realise what you've done?!"

He pulled a soiled handkerchief from his pocket to wrap around his bleeding wound. Realising he had to wash the hand in case of infection, he headed for the bathroom.

The water was cold, and when it collided with his tired face and dripped down his stubble he gave an involuntary shiver. Frank examined his palm and took a long look at his reflection in the mirror.

If only the little cretin hadn't interfered.

Taking a towel, he dried his weary face before tossing it into the pile of dirty laundry that reigned in the corner. He stopped. Something was wrong. His heart skipped a beat as he turned and glanced once more into the glass.

At first, Frank's appearance remained unchanged, then shock mirrored in his eyes as he saw his features age. The face he saw was undeniably his, but it was at least... forty years older. His fingers slowly crawled up his cheeks as the reflection smiled back with glee.

Infant's Fingers

IMBLE fingers ran through albino curls, hung over the forehead of a sightless girl. Diane had been robbed of her sight as a child, not long after her mother had decided to withdraw her from the world. She'd been raised within a religious sect that expected nothing but total obedience.

"You owe it to me," Luna said, spitefully. "He must die for what he has done to me."

Diane had no choice in anything; it had been that way since her father left. She dreamed of finding him, to ask why he'd abandoned her.

"Consider your wish fulfilled," Diane said, with a face that suggested her conscience was uncomfortable. "I will use my gift and wipe his memory from existence."

Inside Rochester city hospital, in the far corner of the maternity ward, Dr. Renee was inspecting the woman that was lying across the examination table.

"Well, Cynthia, you look just about ready to burst! How are you feeling?"

"Oh, I'm absolutely marvellous."

The Doctor grinned, she was used to sarcasm.

"Have you decided on a name?"

"Not yet, but we have a few in mind."

The Doctor smiled and left the room as her husband marched in with a bucket of lilies.

"Hey, honey. How are you doing?"

Cynthia let out a tired sigh. "Why does everyone have to ask me that?"

James kissed his wife's cheek and playfully caressed her raven hair.

"Have you made a decision?"

"I want to call her Lucy, after your mum."

James leaned forward and kissed her forehead.

"Thank you."

Above the Blackburn residence, dark clouds had gathered. A sinister figure stood before a mirror, staring into her reflection. The shapely form that had once been considered beautiful had been replaced by the warped image of a skeletal creature.

Scott lifted a glass of Scotch, sniffed it and took a sip.

"Are you sure you want to go through with this?"

He savoured the taste on his tongue for a few seconds before swallowing.

"The girl is innocent."

Luna opened a wooden box, removed a curiously shaped medallion and hung it around her neck.

Will he have what it takes when the time comes? If he doesn't, he will pay with his life.

"Do you really want to sacrifice your own daughter for the sake of petty vengeance? The past is the past; you can't change it no matter how much you want to."

Scott took another sip of Scotch to calm his nerves.

"Diane doesn't deserve this fate. I beg you to reconsider."

Knowing what was expected of him didn't make the situation any easier. He needed plenty of encouragement to fulfil his duty. The whisky provided the solution.

Scott tried to continue his point, but Luna raised her hand to silence him.

"You are my brother and I love you, but this has to be done. How can I allow a man to break my heart and find happiness? I know that what I've asked of you will test your devotion to myself and the group, but I cannot allow this treachery to go unpunished. Twelve years ago he walked out on me for that harlot and now he thinks he can start a family. No, he must pay. If I can't have him, no one will."

Luna offered Scott her hand, which he accepted with some apprehension.

"Come, my brother. All is prepared."

The two of them walked, hand in hand, down a flight of stairs into a dark cellar. In its centre was a circle made of sand. A group of hooded figures stood around the sacred ground, waiting for Luna to step up to an altar and address the crowd.

"My children, you are extremely privileged, for tonight you shall witness a spectacle that hasn't been seen in 122 years. A goddess will be reborn."

Luna put two hands around a bejewelled chalice and poured its contents down her throat. She swallowed the sweet nectar and wiped her mouth.

"Shall we begin?"

Six disciples began chanting a secret incantation.

Luna raised her hands to the heavens. "Come forth, my daughter!"

Diane stepped out of the darkness into the circle. Her blank face was illuminated by candlelight. She had been stripped of all dignity and left without clothes.

The chanting got louder as the disciples swayed to a more fervent beat.

Diane remained immobile as Scott removed a torch from the nearest wall and walked begrudgingly towards her.

I must accept my destiny.

Luna muttered words in a language that Diane could not understand. Doubt began to creep into her mind as she turned her blind eyes towards the sound of her mother's voice.

"Now!"

Scott hesitated for a split second, but nonetheless obeyed the command of his sister. He thrust the torch towards Diane and the girl ignited in an instant. Several disciples gasped as she burned like a condemned witch at the stake. Not a single scream escaped her lips. She tilted her head back and raised her arms as if embracing the flames. Luna watched with fascination as her daughter anxiously awaited the result of her metamorphosis.

The cruel flames devoured Diane's tender flesh as her defeated frame collapsed. Only a pile of ash remained where the teenage girl had perished. Scott examined the aftermath and gasped as a child emerged. He could tell it was his niece right away; her teenage mind had been transported into an infant's body. The baby didn't cry, it just gazed into his eyes.

"Diane?" Scott asked in a trembling voice.

He had never witnessed anything quite like this. It was like the rebirth of a Phoenix.

Is this what happened to her?

The girl nodded, as if sensing his thoughts.

He covered the baby in a cotton blanket and walked over to the hooded followers. One of them stepped forward and removed the cape. Scott placed the baby in her arms.

"You know what to do."

The woman bowed in acknowledgement and walked out of the cellar. It was Dr. Renee.

Cynthia blissfully slept in the hospital room, participating in the deepest sleep she'd had in nine months. The birth had been a complete success. James sat by his sleeping wife and admired her loveliness. Even after enduring one of the most traumatic experiences of her life, she was still beautiful.

Dr. Renee walked in and disturbed his train of thought.

"How are you feeling?"

He smirked in amusement, remembering his wife's annoyance with that particular question.

"I'm fine, thank you. How's Lucy?"

Dr. Renee reassured him that little Lucy was doing just fine.

"Tell you what, Cynthia should awake any moment. How about I go and get your daughter, so when she opens her eyes you can be together?"

She beamed and left the room once more. When her foot crossed the threshold, the smile vanished. She walked down the bright corridor and into the newborn room. Inside, the hectic noise of baby cries made her sick. Spending most her career delivering these things had made her despise every single one of them.

Dr. Renee strolled among the rows of newborns. All of them were asleep or crying, except one. This baby possessed an unusually penetrating gaze and an unmistakeable intelligence lurked behind her grey eyes.

After checking that no one was looking, she tied a nametag around the infant's ankle. It read: Lucy Horn. She picked the baby up in her sturdy arms and looked deep into its hypnotic eyes.

"Do it tonight. Nod twice if you can understand me."

The baby girl studied the woman's mouth for a few seconds as if reading her lips, before nodding twice.

"Here we are! Dr. Renee said as she placed the baby into Cynthia's eager arms. "Say hello to your new daughter, Lucy."

"Isn't she gorgeous?" Cynthia asked, full of pride.

"She gets the good looks from her mum."

James kissed his wife's forehead before embracing his newborn daughter.

I'm going to love this little girl more than anything else in this world. If only my other one wasn't such a freak. No! Cynthia must never know. Lucy is the only one! I will love her with all my heart.

As he looked up, the baby's newly opened eyes met his.

"Look, she's smiling at you," Cynthia said. Her voice was full of joy

"Of course she is. She recognizes her daddy."

After two days in the hospital, the little girl called Lucy was peacefully sleeping in her room, in a cot painted with flowers and the rising sun. James was sitting on his bed, reading one of his favourite historical novels by the mercer lamp. He was nervous about being left alone with his new daughter.

What if something goes wrong? Am I capable of handling an emergency if it presents itself?

James put down his book and rolled the silk covers to one side as he silently tip-toed towards the cot to check on Lucy for the twenty-sixth time. The baby was asleep. He walked back to his bed and switched off the light, having finally decided to get some sleep.

As his eyes closed, another pair opened. The baby climbed out of its cot and sneaked towards the kitchen. She picked up a large kitchen knife with both hands, her miniature fingers struggling to hold the weapon. After a few seconds, she settled for a smaller one.

The task was almost finished.

Mother will be so proud!

The baby placed the cold blade on her father's throat. For a moment, the infant hesitated. James' eyes flew open, but in that instant the baby girl slashed his neck with all her strength. It was enough as the knife was sharp. He felt a sudden pain and immediately gasped for breath. The cut was deep, mortally so.

He felt the warm blood pouring down his body onto the sheets. He tried calling for help, but no words escaped his lips.

He gazed into the eyes of the infant, who kneeled on his chest, her grimace triumphant. James looked at her with more intensity than ever before. Suddenly, in his last seconds of life, he recognized something in that malicious stare.

Lifting his hand with the last of his strength, he reached towards the baby's face and caressed her chubby cheek.

"Diane. . . ?"

At last she understood the real deception; she'd just killed her biological father.

"Daddy. . . ?"

Broken Glass

HAT cursed memory constantly haunts me, everywhere I go. Most nights, her pleading lips appear before me, whispering in the dark. She was relying on me and I'd failed her, that much was clear. I still remember the shock and the horror spreading across her face.

I was barely thirteen when it happened. Being a witless pupil of teenage rebellion, the possibility of inflicting harm on another human being had never really occurred to me.

Then it did.

My life was never the same after *the* event. I've always found it kind of ironic how a split second decision could alter my entire destiny; all those years ahead of me, wrecked by a single act.

The desire to hang myself used to invade my mind when I recalled what happened that day. I got away with it, but even though my body is free of the crime, my conscience is not. I'm nothing more than a blank spectre roaming the physical realm.

I was strolling aimlessly, my hands tucked deep in my pockets, along the windy riverbank in Chatham. My mind was preoccupied by the promise of adventure. I should have known of the consequences the day would unravel.

Mark's disintegrating house was only ten minutes from mine. I rang his doorbell eagerly. His mother, Sonia, opened the door and invited me in with the most welcoming smile. She offered me a glass of lemonade which I took gratefully, never dropping my gaze from her enigmatic eyes.

She wore one of those white summer blouses, her gigantic breasts pressed against the soft fabric, begging to be unleashed.

"What have you got planned for today then, Joseph?"

Snapping out of my reverie, I took a sip of the ice cold drink. I hated being addressed by my first name. Everyone knew I liked to be called J.

I returned her warm smile and said in a matter of fact tone: "We will probably go down to the river and hang out."

"That's nice," she replied. "Listen, I want to ask you something. Can you take Jane with you? Just for a few hours. I've been called into work unexpectedly, and I'd rather not leave her in the house alone."

My face turned to stone. Jane, who was only nine at the time, was Mark's younger sister. She suffered from Autism. Her mood swings were something to behold as she was like a hurricane when one of her violent fits took control.

Excuses raced through my mind, but I couldn't think of anything appropriate. "Sure," I said, "but... isn't she... lethal?"

Sonia giggled sweetly. "No. I'm going to give her some medication before you go. Mark knows what to do if she goes berserk. Just be careful and watch out for traffic."

Mark suddenly burst into the room and banged a carton of milk on the table. "There!" he said and stormed off. I chuckled and loyally followed him.

I used to marvel at how devoid of personality his room was. He had an antique bed and a dark brown writing desk. There was no TV or even a radio. No books for Christ's sake.

"Did you know your Mother wants you to take Jane with us?"

"She told me this morning!" Mark replied as he changed into his grey tracksuit pants and a worn t-shirt with a massive hole under his left armpit.

"Why do I have to take my lunatic sister everywhere I go?"

"I don't think what she has classifies as a mental illness. It's more of a... personality defect."

The corner of Mark's mouth cracked into a smile. "Mum thinks I can handle her, but I haven't got a clue."

I felt sorry for him. Who wants to spend their days nursing younger siblings? Thank god I was an only child.

"Look, don't worry about it... we'll go down to the river and play a few games in our secret hideout. She can just sit and watch. Anyway, isn't she sort of catatonic under meds?"

After collecting Jane, we hastily crossed several crowed streets. As we descended the uneven stairs of a bridge, heading towards a path covered by poplar trees, a dead sparrow suddenly fell before me. It just crashed down and landed at my feet. It twitched for a moment and then lay still. My heart skipped a beat as I pondered its symbolic meaning.

Dark clouds were gathering above my head, there was a dusty scent in the atmosphere as the wind picked up. I regretted not wearing something warmer.

Finally, reaching our chosen spot, we sat down on a huge log near a stream. Jane hadn't said a word the entire time, which was fine with us as that's just how we liked her. Silent.

Mark stood up and started exploring. "Hey look at this!" he suddenly exclaimed. I got up lazily and went over to take a peek. "Nice one, Mark!" I said in a mocking tone. "You've found a piece of broken glass."

He seemed disappointed. "For a minute, I thought I'd found an ancient artefact."

"I'm going for a piss," I said, shaking my head in amusement. Jane simply sat there, preoccupied with her own thoughts.

Upon my return, however, I saw her standing behind him. She had a murderous grin on her face. It was then that I saw something sharp in her diminutive hands. The object was being pointed towards Mark's kidneys.

I shouted instinctively: "WATCH OUT!! SHE'S GOING TO STAB YOU!"

He turned around and stared at her. I stood rooted to the spot as she moved gently past him and threw the glass innocently into the calm river.

For a second, no one dared to breathe. "You idiot!" Mark screamed. "You scared me half to death!"

"I'm sorry," I said, panting. "It genuinely looked as if she intended on stabbing you. I overreacted."

The panic was over. We didn't say a lot for a long while, then our eyes met and we broke into laughter.

"Did you really think my own sister was going to kill me?"

"Well, how was I supposed to interpret the situation? I came back and saw her standing behind you with a piece of broken glass. Not to mention her history of violence. So yes, I honestly thought she was going to murder you."

Mark smiled and poked Jane playfully in the ribs. "No, she wouldn't hurt me. She just likes to stand close to people, don't you sis?" She beamed but said nothing.

"I'm really touched by your concern, by the way," Mark said sincerely. "I'm glad we found one another. When I met you in fourth grade, I instantly knew I'd made a friend for life." He extended his hand, which I shook with a warm feeling in my heart.

"Same here," I said. "You're like the brother I never had."

To break the sentimentality of the moment, Mark suggested we play a game. "Tell you what, how about we play a game of who can throw a piece of glass the furthest?"

"Go on, Jane," I said, handing her a frag-
ment I'd retrieved from the dirt. "Since you
gave me and your brother such a massive
scare today, you can go first. Don't cut your-
self though."

She got to her feet and took the glass
from my palm. After spending a few seconds watching the miniature waves on the
river's surface, she stretched her arm out
and threw it. There was a tiny "splash" in
the distance. Jane clapped her hands. Mark
bent down and took a piece himself. "I'll show
you how it's done," he boasted, throwing the
shard much further that his sister had managed. A winning smirk spread across his
bony face.

Never one to back down from a challenge,
I took the final piece and went right to the
edge of the river. "Bet I can throw it to the
other shore," I said. Mark looked at me scep-
tically. "Yeah, right."

We were both so absorbed in the moment
that we forgot about Jane.

That's when it happened.

I stretched out my arm and felt the slippery glass leaving my fingers, but it never
reached the other shore. It never fell into
the water. Instead, I heard a tiny gasp and
turned around.

I'd slashed an artery in Jane's neck, and
now she was gasping for breath. Her left

hand was applying pressure to the exposed flesh while the other was reaching out to me. I just stood there, staring, watching her bleed.

Mark reacted with sense and took off his shirt, pressing it hard against the wound. Her helpless eyes clashed with the surprise in mine. But what did I do? What was my heroic contribution? I ran.

It remains a mystery to me why I decided to take this course of action. I just panicked and bolted as fast as my skinny legs would carry me. Attempting to save her life wasn't an option at the time, letting her die seemed much more appealing. That's the kind of unsympathetic entity I turned out to be.

The darkest corner of my soul longs to tell you that I accompanied her through every stage of suffering and that it was me who dramatically saved her young life, but I disappeared like a line of cocaine before a junkie.

In the months that followed, I searched for an explanation that would justify my cowardly reaction, but I never found one. I just ran home and told my mum what had happened. She called Mark's parents and drove them to the hospital while I hid in the closet and wept like a new born infant.

Mark was the uncompromising hero that day. Not me. Jane survived, but naturally, all communication between us ceased. I wanted to write him a letter, to explain why I'd reacted in such a degrading fashion, but I never found the right words. I could have made up some pathetic excuse, I suppose. I could have said that I'd run for help, but we both knew that was a lie.

Running was my way of dealing with the unpleasant problem that we were forced to confront. Deep down inside of me, hid a rabble of doubts and fears. That's the truth of this horrific account. I've lived with this memory for three months now, and it doesn't get any easier.

I've asked my parents to let me transfer to a different school. "Time is a healer," they said. "It will soon be forgotten."

It wasn't.

Every day, the shame became more and more unbearable. I'd see her in school, her accusing eyes staring into mine as I tried not to look at the horrendous scar that was an eternal symbol of my own cowardice.

But in these last few rainy days, at last a new solution has presented itself. It is one that will erase all suffering. There will be no more shame. No more pain. No more memories.

I'm sitting at my desk, and the rope feels strong in my hand.

I hope the beam holds.

On the Edge of the Marsh

 T dawn, we reached our cabin by the lake. The place that Olivia and I would call home for the next few days. I opened a window and inhaled deeply, taking in the scent of winter. The wind whispered something, but I wasn't listening.

"Isn't this beautiful?"

"It's very pretty, Daddy," my daughter replied, her eyes full of the kind of wonder I remembered having when I was a child.

I retrieved our suitcases from the back of the Jeep. The steps leading up to the cabin creaked under the extra weight. As promised, the key was beneath the welcome mat, but I didn't need to use it. The door was already unlocked. While I doubted there was anything of value inside the property, surely the owner wouldn't have intentionally left it this way?

Cautiously, I stepped inside. My instinct told me that something was very wrong. I looked around, searching for clues. Nothing seemed to be amiss. All I could see was pieces of old furniture coated in dust and thick cobwebs.

"What is it, Dad?"

"Shh!"

I stood for a moment, listening to the silence. It was then that I saw something lurking in the shadows. A hand suddenly reached out and took a hold of mine.

"My name is Logan. I'm your guide."

The intruder stepped out of the darkness into full view. I could see that he possessed a robust frame and dark eyes that glowed despite the absence of light. The man must have been in his early fifties, but he was well preserved. I had no idea what to make of him or what his intentions were. All I knew was that the place was meant to be empty.

"Look, we didn't book any guide. There must have been some kind of mistake."

He smiled but didn't say anything.

"Have you at least got some kind of identification?"

For some reason, the question seemed to amuse him. He laughed as if I'd said something funny. I couldn't think what.

"This is Spirit Lake, friend, we have no need for such things."

"Well, I mean you no disrespect, sir, but if you can't prove who you are, I'll have to ask you to leave. My daughter and I have travelled through the night, and we really need to get some sleep. Perhaps we can revisit this later?"

"Okay," he replied. "I'll see you in a couple of hours."

As he descended the steps, his eyes drifted back towards Olivia. I thought I saw the corner of his mouth rise into a twisted smile. Then he was gone.

My daughter and I sat down at a table which I'd cleaned with a dirty rag I'd found in the sink. We ate a modest breakfast, consisting of ham sandwiches and fruit. I made some coffee, as there was no way I was going to sleep. Olivia was barely able to stand, so I decided to put her to bed, for a couple of hours at least.

Suddenly, there was a loud knock at the door which made us jump. I tiptoed to the window and tried to look out, but I couldn't see a thing. It was so grey that I was sure a storm was coming.

I opened the door, slowly. At first I couldn't see anyone. It was then that I felt someone watching me. Logan. He was leaning against the cabin wall, his face unreadable.

"Are you ready?"

I wanted to tell him to get the hell out of here and go back to wherever he came from, but I figured that maybe if we let him show us around the damn lake, he would go away.

I told him to wait.

Inside the cabin, Olivia was sat on the edge of her bed. All the colour had drained from her face. I could tell she was frightened.

"Put your shoes on," I said. "We're going for a walk."

I reached into my suitcase and pulled out a small hunting knife which I hid in one of my socks. Its presence was enough to reassure the both of us as we left the relative sanctuary of the cabin to meet our guide.

"There is something odd about this place," Logan said, shaking his head as he spoke.

"What do you mean?" I asked.

"When I walk through here at night, I hear strange noises."

Above our heads, the sky began to rumble and rain started to fall, forming tiny bubbles on the surface of the water. It was as if the whole area had stirred because attention had been drawn to it.

Logan pointed towards the marshes. "See!"

My eyes followed his finger. Olivia was staring as intently as I was.

In the distance, there was the sound of an engine. Sure enough, a huge truck was approaching. A large woman dressed in a long coat jumped from her vehicle and strolled over to us.

"Hi," she said, extending her hand. "I'm Emma Gardner. I work for the Mental Institution down the road."

"I'm Ethan. This is my little girl, Olivia. We've rented the cabin for the weekend."

She smiled and nodded her head.

"What can we do for you?" I asked.

"Well, it's a delicate issue," she said. "One of our patients has run off."

I froze.

"Oh, don't worry, he's not dangerous. As with most of our patients, he's just delusional. We like to give them a lot of freedom, but sometimes they do stray from the hospital grounds. You haven't seen anybody suspicious around here, have you?"

"Well, there was an intruder in our cabin. He called himself Logan."

"Could you describe him?"

"He's about 6'4, with greyish hair and a dark beard. He's actually right over there. . . "

I turned around, but our friend had already gone.

"You know, you really should take better care of those under your charge. They shouldn't be allowed to wander around regular folk. I mean, this weirdo frightened my daughter. . . and me!"

"I assure you, he is quite harmless. John wouldn't hurt a fly. Everyone knows Mr. Kovak in this town, so I'm sure we'll find him sooner or later."

The woman didn't seem to be unduly troubled by the fact that one of her inmates was free to cause havoc. This was the final straw, the end of our vacation. I took Olivia by the hand and started walking back to the cabin.

That was when the thought hit me. John Kovak? Who the hell was Logan?

Affectionate Cadaver

 N the day my Father was returned to the earth, I knew something was wrong with me. Whilst my relatives were crying for the dearly departed, I was delighting in the company of my own melancholy. I began to develop an appreciation for the macabre. Having realised that I shared more in common with the dead than the living, I decided that I needed to be in the company of corpses.

Three weeks after the funeral, I applied for a job as a mortician's assistant. No experience was required, only a willing heart and sincere attitude.

I worked under the supervision of Mr. Wilkes. He made no secret of his dislike for me. From the first day I met him, it was clear he despised me. The feeling was mutual.

During my first week, a body went missing, only to reappear two days later. Nobody could explain how or why it had happened, but the suspicion fell entirely on me.

I knocked on a solid mahogany door and entered after a slight pause. Mr. Wilkes was sitting behind his marble desk, gesturing for me to sit in the leather chair opposite him. He studied my face as we sat in silence.

"Do you know why I've summoned you here?"

"No, Sir."

"I have reason to believe that you were involved in the theft of a corpse. As a consequence of your debauched act of thievery, we have decided to dismiss you with immediate effect."

I felt the blood drain from my face. "I don't understand? I don't know anything about a missing body. I'm new here."

Mr. Wilkes would not have any of my protestations. My guilt had already been decided.

"If you sign this," he said, passing me a piece of headed paper, "I'll let you call it a resignation. This will help you avoid any awkward questions."

I hesitated, but it was obvious that I didn't have a choice. I had to concede.

Mr. Wilkes shook his head in disgust.

"I..."

He held his hand up as if to silence me. I was already lost for words to defend myself with.

"I don't want to know," he said. "You're sick!"

I nodded and offered a hand that he refused to shake. It didn't matter to him that I was innocent. He wanted to believe that it was me. I was forced to retreat.

Dusk had already descended by the time I left the building. I could hear the rustling of leaves in the autumn breeze as I walked through the deserted car park towards my 1978 Cherokee. As I switched on the engine, a sense of bitterness overwhelmed me.

Why am I the one that is always rejected?

I had to take a risk and prove to myself that I wasn't a failure.

Kathryn was my neighbour. I found her attractive but knew I had no chance. I was always too shy to make an impression on her. She had this reputation for being easy, which intimidated me. For some reason, tonight was different. I invited her over. To my surprise, she accepted the offer.

I've had a few girlfriends over the years, but my relationships always seem to end in tears. They turn sour for reasons that have never been explained to me. In the end, I stopped trying. I buried myself in books and slipped into the dark realms they offered.

There was a knock at the door. I hesitated, but knew who it was.

For a moment, I sat in silence, contemplating what to do next. I'd resolved to remain single, yet I was about to entertain a woman. I consoled myself with the idea that all I had to do was serve wine and make polite conversation.

A vision of beauty stood before me. I looked into her ocean-blue eyes and imagined the touch of her delicate mouth against mine.

"Would you like to come in?"

I didn't hear her answer. My attention was arrested by her breasts and the erect nipples that were protruding from her blouse. My knees began to tremble as I began to think impure thoughts.

I offered her a glass of wine before pouring my own.

"Sit down," she said, patting the couch suggestively. "You don't have to be shy around me."

I did as I was told.

"How's your love life?"

"Non-existent," I said, truthfully. My eyes wandered to her blouse again.

"How about yours?"

A mischievous smile spread across Kathryn's face as she playfully ran her fingers through her hair. She giggled and placed her hand on my thigh. My whole body stiffened. I could feel my manhood swelling inside my trousers.

"So you're not seeing anyone at the moment?"

"Not right now," I said. "I'm still waiting on that special someone, you know? I'm looking for a woman to complete me. What about you?"

"I haven't had much luck with men to be honest. . . you seem different."

Kathryn's hand began to stroke my thigh, and I was unable to resist the temptation any longer. I sat the glass down on the table and leaned in for a kiss. She let out a soft moan and parted her lips, allowing my tongue to slip inside her mouth. My trembling hand snaked its way beneath her blouse, but just as I began to enjoy myself, she suddenly pulled away.

"I'm so sorry, Alfred. This wine is making me dizzy!" She blushed and looked away like a naughty schoolgirl. "I'm not sure this is such a good idea."

I sat on the couch, motionless. Then, an overwhelming desire took a hold of me. I felt silent rage rising within.

No, not again. Not this time. I won't be rejected.

I decided to wipe that seductive smile from her face and summon my only friend and ally. . . death.

My hands wrapped themselves around Kathryn's slender neck. She gasped and struggled for breath, but my grip on her throat only tightened. As I strangled her, I felt the euphoria of having power over another life. I felt like a god.

Sadly, it was over sooner than expected. I kneeled over her lifeless body, expecting to feel remorse, but when I looked deep into her hollow eyes, I felt nothing.

I stared at her for what seemed like an eternity, admiring her beautiful features. Yes, even in death she retained her attraction.

Why did you have to reject me?

I picked up her frail body and carried it into the bedroom. Placing her on the stained mattress, I stroked her curls and sat down beside her. I unbuttoned her blouse and exposed her breasts before climbing on top of her lifeless body. I bent down and kissed her neck before allowing my tongue to explore the rest of Kathryn's body.

I reached over to the bedside cabinet and pulled a small plastic jar out of the first drawer. I parted her legs and smeared a generous portion of Vaseline between her sheaths before letting myself in.

Her body was still warm as I rhythmically moved inside her, slowly at first and then more vigorously. I rubbed her breasts and kissed her mouth, moaning with every movement. I climaxed quickly and collapsed on top of her cadaver.

"Thank you," I whispered in her ear. "You were wonderful."

Dear reader,

We hope you enjoyed reading *Moribund Tales*.
Please take a moment to leave a review, even
if it's a short one. Your opinion is important
to us.

Discover more books by Erik Hofstatter at
https://www.nextchapter.pub/authors/erik-
hofstatter

Want to know when one of our books is free
or discounted? Join the newsletter at
http://eepurl.com/bqqB3H

Best regards,
Erik Hofstatter and the Next Chapter Team

 RIK Hofstatter is a dark fiction writer, who dwells in a beauteous and serenading Garden of England, where he can be frequently encountered consuming reckless amounts of mead and tyrannizing local peasantry.

At a young age, he built a Viking ship and journeyed myriad sea miles away from native land in search of plunder and pillage. His work appeared in various magazines and anthologies around the world such as: Schlock, The Strange and the Curious, Inner Sins, Sanitarium and Psychopomp. Erik's axe is a loyal companion and never departs its master's side. More information can be found on his website,

Moribund Tales
ISBN: 978-4-86752-948-5 (Mass Market)

Published by
Next Chapter
1-60-20 Minami-Otsuka
170-0005 Toshima-Ku, Tokyo
+818035793528
12th August 2021